THOMAS ON THE MOON

Illustrated by DRi Artworks
Cover illustration by Tommy Stubbs

 A GOLDEN BOOK · NEW YORK

Thomas the Tank Engine & Friends™

CREATED BY BRITT ALLCROFT

Based on the Railway Series by the Reverend W Awdry
© 2001 Gullane (Thomas) LLC. Cover art copyright © 2017 Gullane (Thomas) LLC.
Thomas the Tank Engine & Friends and Thomas & Friends are trademarks of Gullane (Thomas) Limited.
Thomas the Tank Engine & Friends and Design Is Reg. U.S. Pat. & Tm. Off. © 2017 HIT Entertainment
Limited. All rights reserved. Published in the United States by Golden Books, an imprint of Random House
Children's Books, a division of Penguin Random House LLC, 1745 Broadway, New York, NY 10019, and
in Canada by Penguin Random House Canada Limited, Toronto. Originally published in different form by
Random House Children's Books, New York, in 2001. Golden Books, A Golden Book, A Little Golden Book,
the G colophon, and the distinctive gold spine are registered trademarks of Penguin Random House LLC.
ISBN 978-0-399-55853-5 (trade) — ISBN 978-0-399-55854-2 (ebook)
randomhousekids.com
www.thomasandfriends.com
Printed in the United States of America
10 9 8 7 6 5 4 3 2 1
Random House Children's Books supports the First Amendment and celebrates the right to read.

Thomas was very excited. Today was the opening of the big Space Fair in the park. Sir Topham Hatt had asked Thomas to take the schoolchildren through the exhibits.

The children all talked at once. Thomas could see that they were as excited as he was.

"I love everything about space," Thomas said. "Someday I'd like to go there."

"Thomas in space! How silly!" The children giggled at that thought.

There were many exhibits at the Space Fair.
Thomas waited patiently for the children at each one.

Thomas wondered what it would be like
to shoot through space like a rocket.

The group came to a field, where the planets of
the solar system were displayed in their proper order.

MAR

In the center was the sun. The two planets closest
to the sun were Mercury and Venus.

Next was Earth, the third planet from the sun.
"Let's see if we can find the Island of Sodor!" the
children said with excitement.

A friendly guide offered
to tell the children more.

"Jupiter is the largest planet in our solar system," she explained. "It's bigger than all the other planets put together. Mercury is the smallest. On Mercury the sky is always black!"

Everybody loved the model of Saturn, with its beautiful rings of ice.

By this time, the children were hungry.

"Space is a beautiful place for a picnic," peeped Thomas as he brought the sandwiches.

The guide talked some more about space. "If you could ride Thomas to the sun," she said, "it would take almost two hundred years to get there!"

After lunch, the guide demonstrated how planets travel around the sun. Thomas got to be the sun. The boys and girls took their places as planets and circled around Thomas.

Everyone got to see what it would be like to walk on Mars. Mars has volcanoes that are taller than any mountain on Earth.

After that, the children saw the most amazing display of all—a real moon rock!

"How did that get here?" one of the girls asked.

Then the group heard a familiar *peep*.

"Look, everybody!" one of the boys called.
He laughed. "It's Thomas on the moon!"

That night, Sir Topham Hatt came by to check on Thomas.

"I heard that you had quite a day," he said.

"Yes, Sir!" Thomas said. He sighed happily and closed his eyes. *After all,* he thought, *I've been all the way to the moon and back!*